Unicorn Playlist

Another Phoebe and Her Unicorn Adventure

Complete Your Phoebe and Her Unicorn Collection

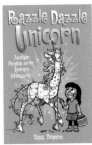

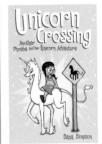

Unicorn Playlist

Another Phoebe and Her Unicorn Adventure

Dana Simpson

Andrews McMeel
PUBLISHING®

Hey, kids!

Check out the glossary starting on page 173
if you come across words you don't know.

I know what it is like to be sad for no reason.

Yeah... but this different.

Today I'm sad about *EVERYTHING.*

My dad left a news site up on his laptop and I SAW what adults are doing these days.

I am so sorry.

Everything is bad except unicorns.

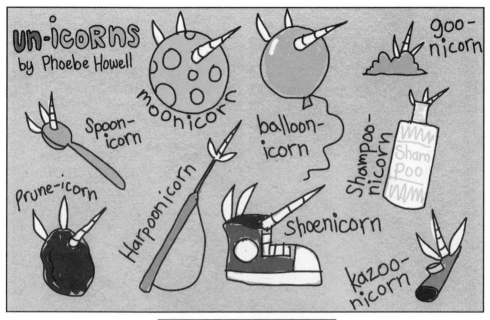

My parents say a lot more useful stuff used to come in the mail.

It is similar for unicorns.

In the days before modern unicorn communication, we used to use an elegant system known as...

Lemme guess.

The "Pony Express"?

The *"POINTY* Express."

The *Pointy Express* was a primitive but effective means of sending messages over long distances.

It enabled us to get messages to unicorns on the far side of the world in just days, without any one unicorn having to travel too far.

NEIGH!

poke

Lilyflanks Appleblossom is having a Sparkle Day Party.

I will tell the next unicorn! Have fun gazing at yourself!

Each unicorn finds another unicorn, pokes them with their horn, and relays the message.

Then, that unicorn finds the next unicorn to poke, and the chain continues.

Sometimes, I miss the old ways, before horn wi-fi. They had a certain...simple elegance.

Getting poked in the butt with a horn has a "simple elegance"?

I never said "butt." It is not my fault if you chose to picture that.

15

It's part of how unicorns communicated in OLDEN times!

Modern times are way better.

That was actually my point.

I have a new favorite song!

I heard it online last night.

It goes "da da DAAAA da da daaaaa..."

"DOOT da DOOT da DOOT DOOT"...

I will take your word for it.

Imagine the "doots" are cool synth stings.

It's a nice day, for November. Shouldn't you be out for a ride with Marigold?

She doesn't like a song as much as I do, so now I'm questioning whether I even FEEL like going for a unicorn ride today.

Okay, now that I say that out loud...

As your mom, I have to take your feelings seriously, but yeah, go ride your unicorn.

I have a song I would like to share with YOU now.

This is a MAGIC MUSICAL PYRAMID. It is an ancient unicorn method of musical storage.

Unicorns feel that all worthwhile magical objects should come to a point.

What about scrolls?

They sort of have corners. We have decided that counts.

Here. My dad says EVERYBODY will agree on THIS music.

Dad says most people agree on the Beatles.

He also said we should play it on vinyl because it would sound better.

For the record, I can also do this with CDs.

Dad says it's not as warm a sound.

Hey unicorn.

Yes?

Prunella sent me a text. You know. The, like, Goblin Queen.

I need you to translate this text she sent me.

She says she can no longer tolerate your efforts to outshine her, and challenges you, once and for all, to a *popularity contest*.

I don't believe you that "BLÄRT" says all that.

It is a very meaningful umlaut.

I'm not even TRYING to outshine the Goblin Queen! I'm just, y'know, existing.

'S not MY fault I'm cooler than her.

As a unicorn, I sympathize. We the fabulous often suffer.

If you mean to win this popularity contest, I offer my services as a POPULARITY COACH.

...are YOU popular with other unicorns?

I am not on trial here.

The way goblin popularity contests work is, first you walk ten paces.

Then, you will be scanned with a popularity meter, which will decide this contest.

Why the paces then?

They saw it in a Western and thought it seemed cool.

Popularity contests are stupid.

THANK you.

Are you sure you even WANT to be popular with goblins? You don't seem to like them all that much.

I DON'T. They're weird and gross and their language sounds like burping.

But I like being popular even with lesser beings. Isn't that why your unicorn hangs out with YOU?

NO.

Indeed! She is bribing me with apples.

The key, Dakota, is BELIEVING you are popular. It is a state of mind. It is something you project.

I know that! Tell me something I DON'T know!

"Dakota" is an ancient unicorn word meaning "nose lice"!

It IS?

No! Which is how I knew you did not know it.

This is unicorn humor.

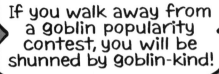

If you walk away from a goblin popularity contest, you will be shunned by goblin-kind!

Goblins will no longer follow you around. They will not carry you to and from school.

They will *totally ghost* you.

Whatever.

Here. I'll put the plunger on MY head.

She does so regularly, as part of her famous impression of me.

Perhaps one day, Dakota will find a magical friend who truly suits her.

For now, it is wise of her to choose to spend some time alone.

You mean apart from her usual throng of human friends?

Do you think I should isolate her in a secluded magical dimension for a few days?

Let's wait until the week of auditions for the school play.

dana

"Robin Hood" is an old human legend? But there are no humans at all in this story, so far.

♪ Oo de lally, oo de lally

Well, this is the ANIMAL version of it. Sometimes humans like stories that AREN'T about us.

Unicorns like stories about unicorns.

I just picture every character I like in a movie as me!

How do you picture the characters you DON'T like?

Me, but wearing a very stupid hat.

I keep thinking about that "Robin Hood" legend.

Unicorns have a similar legendary figure!

That fellow who robbed from the rich, and gave to the poor.

He is called *Coriander Featherhat*. Legend has it he robbed from unicorns with a large number of sparkly things.

My jewels! How uncouth!

And gave them to unicorns with FEWER sparkly things?

No, he just hid them so he would not need to wear sunglasses so much.

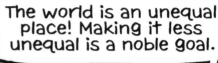

I find myself inspired by this Robin Hood fellow.

The world is an unequal place! Making it less unequal is a noble goal.

Thus shall I become... *THE DOER OF JUSTICE.*

I could call you "D.J." for short!

No, everyone would confuse me with my cousin Daffodil Jauntyflanks.

Can YOU see anything when I'm sparkling this much?

It is a small price to pay for justice to be served.

CRUNCH

From the sound of it, now justice is blind AND stuck.

I stand by my principles.

Until your sparkles go back down, these magic sunglasses will protect us.

But I do not want to have to wear sunglasses.

I suppose in that way, I am more Coriander Featherhat than Robin Hood.

But make no mistake...

THE DOER OF JUSTICE shall ride again!

Your costume should have sequins!

SEQUINS?? Have we learned NOTHING?!

Having trouble shopping for the unicorn who has everything? Let us help once again, with another

UNICORN
HOLIDAY GIFT GUIDE

Horn mistletoe

Now you owe me a kiss!

All right, but you must lower your head due to my great humility.

Technically, it's a decoration. The gift is what you get BECAUSE of it.

Contrast

I feel even lovelier standing next to a non-unicorn!

Sometimes the best gifts are the easiest!

Personal ballad

Pretty much all unicorns like it when you sing their praises!

Unicorn mittens

No they are not just glorified socks.

Friendship, again

Your unicorn won't complain that it's also what you got her last year!

We could talk about shopping, or Santa, or snow
Or stars on the treetop, and tinsel below
We could sing all the carols that everyone knows
Or check on the TV for holiday shows
But for me, the best moment the day can bestow
Is to sit with my presents in unicorn glow.

"Lord Splendid Humility."

Oh, dear.

I must have given him your present, and you his, by mistake! I wonder why he has not said anything.

You are wearing a gold second horn that says "Phoebe."

Having two horns and a human name makes me weird, and therefore humble.

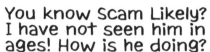

I am making a *FORMAL DECLARATION of RESOLUTION* for this, the forthcoming human annum.

What's an "annum"?

It is an old human word for "year."

If you're gonna use words I don't know, why not UNICORN words?

The unicorn word for that is "neigh."

That means like thirty different things.

I am TRYING to make a *formal declaration* here.

In recent years, I have made, and kept, a resolution to be magnificent, which I knew I would be able to keep...

And I have made, and FAILED to keep, a resolution NOT to be magnificent, knowing I would FAIL to keep it, thus curbing my vanity.

This year, I proclaim a resolution I MAY or MAY NOT be able to keep.

Are you going to resolve to start getting to your point quicker?

No, but I shall keep that in mind for next year.

For this new year, I resolve to learn more about my family.

Spending time around you and your parents has made me wish to discover my own family roots.

I, too, wish to have nose-blowing contests with my father, judged by both auditory and physical volume.

That one might be really specific to my family.

No, no... some things are universal.

When we first met, you told me you didn't HAVE parents.

Not so.

You asked if I had parents. I said, "Not that I have ever met."

You DO have parents, then?

Well, I must have come from SOMEWHERE.

Maybe you hatched from an egg!

It would have to be one of those REALLY SPARKLY eggs.

dana

If you don't remember your family, what DO you remember?

School.

All the young unicorns were together at the Sparkle Academy, where we all lived and learned.

My sister was there, but she was the only relative I remember.

And of course we were always very different.

Are my nostrils not heavenly?

I see a booger!

Florence often knows things I do not. She is a bit more...

Curious?

Well, no, I wish to know new things myself.

But whereas Florence will just go look things up in a book, or online...

I prefer to loudly complain that I do not know something until someone takes pity on me and looks it up FOR me.

But now that you told me that, I'm onto you.

You will still look things up for me because you like me so much.

My fourth cousin twice removed is a rather fearsome unicorn.

There are fearsome unicorns?

He is a **VAMPIRE UNICORN.**

His name is *Vlad of the Red Nostrils*. He sucks the juices out of poor defenseless fruit!

BLEH!

That isn't fearsome.

I may have the intonation wrong on "bleh."

I will see if my parents write me back, and go from there.

You've been fine without them until now.

And I will continue to be fine, regardless.

But I will need you to keep me distracted so I do not sit anxiously by the mail tree, nervously chewing my hooves.

That's sort of a gross habit.

It is the flaw that makes me a masterpiece.

You know...I'm friends with my parents, but not everybody is.

Indeed. I hope I like them, but we will see.

They are the family I cannot choose. I will always have my CHOSEN family.

I'm like your weird little sister who sits on you.

I did not realize how much I wanted one of those.

dana

You can't just sit here waiting to see if your parents write you back.

I know, but it is hard to think about anything else.

PPTH BPHT

That WAS somewhat distracting.

That was just my distraction warm-up exercise.

The key to being distracted is to forget you're trying to be distracted.

If you remember you're trying to distract yourself, that makes you think about what you're trying to distract yourself FROM.

You have to think of something your brain finds so all-consuming that it just naturally obsesses!

I will need you to repeat this later.

Nah, you've got it.

I am skeptical that video games will be as distracting as my own image.

Ultra Mega Random Character Battle introduced Princess Rainbow Sparkle as a playable character.

The sparkliest princess in all of video games?

Yup.

Move over and select an inferior character so that I may defeat you.

There's more than one kind of reflection.

Thank you. You have been a wonderful distraction today.

I have scarcely thought about the thing I was trying to forget!

It's what friends do.

Well, it is appreciated, Karen.

Phoebe!

Phoebe. Of course.

You cast a forgetting spell on yourself, didn't you?

I did not expect you to do such a good job.

I am expecting a possible guest this week.

Another relative I recently learned about. My cousin...

INFERNUS, THE UNICORN OF DEATH.

I might just go hide under the bed.

It is an old family name.

INFERNUS, THE UNICORN OF DEATH will be here later today.

I would appreciate it if you would tag along and start the conversation.

Oh, sure.

So, unicorn of death! That must be fun. Tell me about it!

I am in AWE of you as a conversationalist.

Socially, you unicorns coast pretty hard on being unicorns, don't you?

Hi, you must be Cousin Marigold Heavenly Nostrils.

I am Infernus, the Unicorn of Death.

I have to say, you're not what I was expecting.

You can call me "Ferny."

It is good to meet you, Ferny. I have been very curious to meet more of my relatives.

We have all been very curious about you, too.

My father has a saying about your branch of the family.

"The Nostrils family has disappeared up their own nostrils."

He says that, and then he giggles and snorts and stamps his hoof for several minutes.

Psh. Dad jokes.

Here. You, too, are invited!

So all the unicorns can be all like "ha ha, humans look weird"?

I would never!

I think you are as radiant as a thousand stars!

...what?

Nearly as radiant as a unicorn.

What are you doing for the rest of the afternoon?

Mom is taking me to the store to get Valentines to give the kids in my class.

I was gonna make my own, but my mom thought the prototype was in bad taste.

dana

"I do not wish you any specific harm, but we both know I am being forced to give you this."

Hey, *I* used contractions.

Picked some Valentines yet?

I dunno...

I need these to say so much to so many different people.

How do you say "I like you" to Max, "I still have reservations about our friendship" to Dakota, "I don't have any feelings about you at all" to Herkimer...

Do these ones with the caterpillars say that?

There is no Herkimer. He's a composite character.

dana

111

Hey, Phoebe. Thanks for the Valentine.

Well, thanks for yours, too.

WELCOME TO TIPTON ELEMENTARY

I know we have to get them for everyone, but I'd get you one anyway.

So you really mean what it says?

Are you asking if you're really o-FISH-ally my awesomest friend?

Yeah, I'd hate to think you'd lie to me through fish.

INFERNUS, THE UNICORN OF DEATH.

Don't be afraid of Infernus. ...Ferny.

Neigh're just a unicorn I met who I guess likes me.

And I know what you're thinking... "neigh" is a nonbinary unicorn pronoun.

Actually, I was thinking I shouldn't worry so much whether you think I'm weird.

Yeah, you can o-FISH-ally stop worrying.

Why are you taking humility lessons, anyway?

Because...

...I want to make sure you continue to like me.

Aw. That's sweet.

So I decided I should pretend to be unaware of my own unimpeachable, sparkling magnificence.

That's less sweet.

I shall cast a spell upon you, temporarily granting you magic *unicorn nostrils.*

ZAP

Hmm...

Like if someone sprinkled sriracha sauce on clover.

The stallions will scarcely know what hit them.

When I told my mom what we were gonna do today, she said things have changed a lot since she was a kid.

She said none of the boys she knew then would have wanted to be seen having a TEA PARTY with a *GIRL*.

Hey, sort of friend. You should, like, eat lunch at OUR table.

You're formally declaring me cool enough to sit at your table?

Whatever. It's just weird that not all my friends sit at the same table.

Okay, but later I'm gonna make you sign a formal declaration of sufficient coolness.

Just come sit down before I change my mind.

So, like, my mom said I can't use the living room TV for Netflix until I clean my room.

Yeah, MY mom said I have to start making my unicorn stop leaving rainbow-dust hoofprints between the front door and where we keep the Thin Mints.

THERE. *SEE?* THAT was a death stare.

You could at LEAST try as hard to seem normal as the goblins did.

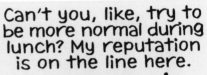

I had lunch with Dakota and her friends.

How'd that go?

Weird.

I'm weird, and you're weird, so together that's normal. But when only one person is weird, it gets WEIRD.

So weird is only weird in odd numbers?

Hey, maybe that's why we CALL them that.

What if Dakota hung out with us this recess?

I dunno.

I'll make her promise to be nice to you.

I'm not sure I can promise to be nice to HER.

Could you be mean in really deadpan ways she won't get?

You know I can.

dana

133

So Dakota tried to introduce me into her friend group, and I tried to introduce her into mine.

Neither really worked.

I guess I just have to hang out with them separately.

While you were doing that, I was on a quest!

I have found the long-lost *Orb of Fortune.*

That sounds a lot more fun.

You seemed busy. I did not want to trouble you with such a minor quest.

Phoebe! You must help me with my humility lessons homework!

I must?

Please! I will help you with YOUR homework later.

Like you helped me with my history report last week?

I made it *SPARKLIER!*

I keep telling you, we're not graded on that.

dana

You must say mean, funny things about me, and I must find it in myself to be genuinely amused.

My homework is to be the subject of a comedy roast, and react with jovial good humor.

You mean I get to say everything mean I've been thinking throughout our entire friendship?!

Um...

I'll clear my calender for the entire week.

Homework is SCARY.

COMEDY ROAST OF MARIGOLD HEAVENLY NOSTRILS

What insulting things can I say about my best friend, Marigold Heavenly Nostrils?

She's...too tall. Like, so tall it makes me feel bad about how short I am.

dana

Do not make this about yourself!

She's a GIGANTIC hypocrite.

Better!

Marigold is SO self-absorbed...

How self-absorbed AM I?

She's SO self-absorbed, she literally absorbed herself and now she's, um, not...there anymore. 'Cause she's in herself.

Look, you gave me 12 minutes to prepare for this comedy roast.

I DO rush people! An excellent roast.

The thing about Marigold is, she's wrong about why people like her.

Why I like her, at any rate.

It's not because she's pretty or magic or a unicorn. It's because she wants to share her pretty magic unicornosity with people. With ME.

Marigold's not actually selfish. At the end of the day, she's the least selfish person I know!

YOU TAKE THAT BACK!!!

When it comes to roasts, I know my audience.

dana

Hey, there's a meteor shower tonight!

We should go look at the stars if it's clear.

It will be clear.

Unicorns can scare away clouds with a **VERY STERN LOOK.**

Then why is it ever cloudy?

Because I do not want my face to get stuck like this.

Ooh, did you see THAT one?

Yeah, that was a good one!

That shooting star, with those five nearby stars, was like a very brief constellation.

James the Caterpillar. A constellation that existed for only a fraction of a second.

Well, now you made it tragic.

My beauty does not show in the dark, so I have to be DEEP.

Are you wishing on any of these shooting stars?

No...unicorns do not get to wish on shooting stars.

You don't?

Tragically not.

That's even more tragic than the caterpillar thing.

Well, it is UNICORN LAW.

Why don't you get to wish on shooting stars?

Because we are already unicorns.

And we do not wish to be selfish. There are a finite number of wishes in the world.

There are?

Every wish is a requested withdrawal from the Bank of Wishes.

It is in Akron, in a magical office park.

And a few more of my childhood illusions die.

dana

My dad says there are other universes, with other Phoebes.

Indeed. There are so many excellent Phoebes.

You've MET them?

Many of them, yes.

Mind... BLOWN.

Ha! That is SUCH a Universe 74B Phoebe thing to say!

Alternate Phoebe will be along at ANY MOMENT. Be prepared!

BWAAAAAAA!

BWAAAAAAAA.

I wasn't PREPARED for this!

Then you should have prepared more!

BWA.

164

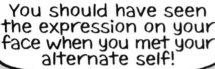

You should have seen the expression on your face when you met your alternate self!

Do you WANT to go and see now?

What?

I and your future self just played an excellent prank on your past self!

We got you to mistake *TIME TRAVEL PHOEBE* for *INTERDIMENSIONAL PHOEBE.*

Ooh, now I want your future self to see THIS expression, too!

So ARE there other Phoebes in other dimensions?

I honestly do not know.

But I like to think so! I like to think an infinite number of Phoebes and Marigolds are trotting together through infinite dimensions.

Maybe there's one where you're a human.

MAYBE THERE IS ONE WHERE *YOU* ARE A HUMAN!!

We need to work on your comebacks.

I panicked.

GLOSSARY

accommodate (uh-kah-muh-date): pg. 108 – verb / to provide for something that is needed, such as housing, money, or any special conditions

blart (blarrrt): pg. 44 – various parts of speech / Goblin-speak for many different kinds of expressions, exclamations, and meanings; hard to translate for anyone who doesn't speak Goblin

Bluetooth (blue-tooth): pg. 157 – noun / a kind of technology through which devices can be paired wirelessly, such as computers, phones, televisions, and speakers

composite (kum-pah-zit): pg. 111 – adjective / made up of different parts or people in a combined form; a composite character is a character constructed of many different people's personality traits

deadpan (ded-pan): pg. 133 – adjective / very flat or expressionless in tone

earworm (ear-worm): pg. 30 – noun / a tune or melody that gets stuck in your head

eccentric (ick-sen-trick): pg. 101 – adjective / quirky or unpredictable in behavior or character

electrolytes (i-leck-tro-lights): pg. 125 – noun / essential minerals and compounds that dissolve in water and help your body produce energy and perform other essential functions

finite (fy-night): pg. 153 – adjective / having an end or a stopping point, not unending

hypocrite (hi-poh-krit): pg. 144 – noun / someone who says one thing and does another

ignominious (ig-nuh-mi-nee-us): pg. 67 – adjective / humiliating and shameful

interpretation (in-tur-pri-tay-shun): pg. 33 — noun / how someone understands or comprehends something

mandolin (man-duh-lin): pg. 22 — noun / a small stringed instrument in the lute family, containing double strings and played with a small pick called a plectrum

marimba (muh-rim-buh): pg. 22 — noun / a percussion instrument with wooden bars struck by rubber mallets, similar to a xylophone but with a softer, more mellow, tone

multiverse (muhl-tee-verse): pg. 158 — noun / a theory that there are a limitless number of universes in which different versions of ourselves exist and make different choices

nonbinary (non-bye-nuh-ree): pg. 115 — adjective / a gender identity that is neither male nor female; many (but not all) nonbinary people use they/them pronouns instead of he/she

Pony Express (poh-nee ik-spres): pg. 13 — noun / a system of mail delivery in America using horseback delivery, in operation between 1860 and 1861

project (pruh-jekt): pg. 43 — verb / to signal or display for an audience

roast (rohst): pg. 145 — noun / an event in which people tell stories or make jokes about someone as a humorous form of tribute

synth (sinth): pg. 20 — noun / short for "synthesizer," an instrument resembling a keyboard that recreates different sounds, which gained popularity in 1980s pop music

umlaut (oom-lout): pg. 38 — noun / an accent mark placed above vowels in languages such as German or Hungarian, symbolized by two small dots; it indicates the way a vowel should be pronounced

vinyl (vie-nuhl): pg. 32 — noun / a format for musical recordings (usually called a "record"), much like a CD except larger and made with a plastic coating

Andrews McMeel Publishing
a division of Andrews McMeel Universal
1130 Walnut Street, Kansas City, Missouri 64106

www.andrewsmcmeel.com

21 22 23 24 25 SDB 10 9 8 7 6 5 4 3 2 1

ISBN: 978-1-5248-6857-4

Library of Congress Control Number: 2021936006

Made by:
King Yip (Dongguan) Printing & Packaging Factory Ltd.
Address and location of manufacturer:
Daning Administrative District, Humen Town
Dongguan Guangdong, China 523930
1st Printing—6/21/21

ATTENTION: SCHOOLS AND BUSINESSES

Andrews McMeel books are available at quantity discounts with bulk purchase for educational, business, or sales promotional use. For information, please e-mail the Andrews McMeel Publishing Special Sales Department: specialsales@amuniversal.com.

Look for these books!

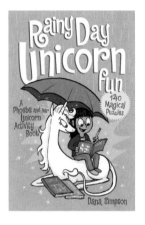

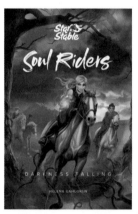